I LOST MY BEAR

JULES FEIFFER

SCHOLASTIC INC.
New York Toronto London Auckland Sydney
Mexico City New Delhi Hong Kong

Watercolor and ink were used for the full-color illustrations. The text type is hand-lettered.

ISBN 0-439-09779-7

12 11 10 9 8 7 6 5 4 3 2 1   9/9 0 1 2 3 4/0

Printed in the U.S.A.   14

First Scholastic printing, September 1999

For Charlotte

UH-OH...

I can't find my bear.

I asked my mother.

I tried to think like a detective and remember where I was playing with it last.

I think I was playing with it last under the bed.

But I don't see it.

Maybe I was playing with it last in the bookcase.

Hmm. I don't see it.

Was I playing with it last in the living room?

It's not on the couch.

Or behind the curtains. It's not under the chairs.

So . . .

I asked my sister.

And she said:

Nobody will help me find my bear.

So I cried.

And nobody stopped me.

So I stopped myself.

But I know it's gone

forever.

My sister said:

But which stuffed animal?

If I throw one of my favorites,
what if I lose that one too?

So I better throw a stuffed animal
I don't care about.

But if I pick one I don't care about,
it will know.

And it won't want to find my lost bear.

EENY MEENY MINEY MO-
INK A BINK A BOTTLE OF INK-

1 POTATO 2 POTATO 3 POTATO 4-
I CHOOSE YOU!

My bunny rabbit is my second favorite stuffed animal after my bear.

I can't do it!

I go to my sister.

I have the best sister in the world!

I closed my eyes.

And I threw it!

And it found my lost barrette.

Then it found my lost kitten.

But she wasn't really lost, she was hiding.

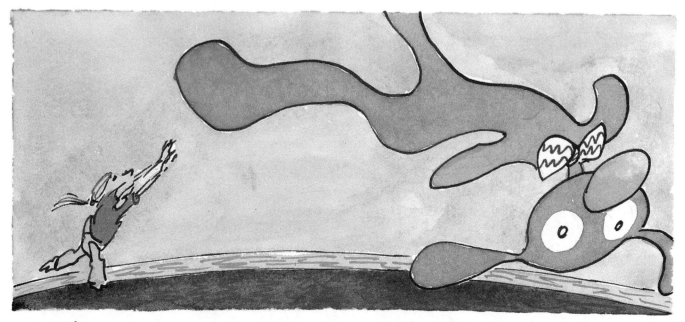

Then it found my lost Magic Markers.

So I drew a picture of my lost bear.

Then . . .

my one last extra-special-I-really-mean-it-this-time throw.

It found my lost purse.

And inside my purse was a bunch of other things I lost.

So I played with them.

Until bedtime ...

When my mother said:

IT'S TIME FOR BED. DID YOU FIND YOUR LOST BEAR?

OH, MY GOSH! I forgot all about my bear!

I cried.

Because I was ashamed I forgot about my bear.

Aren't I the best detective?